THE BOY
WHO OWNED
THE SCHOOL

THE BOY WHO OWNED THE SCHOOL

A Comedy of Love by

GARY PAULSEN

A Little Yearling Book

Published by
Dell Publishing
a division of
Bantam Doubleday Dell Publishing Group, Inc.
666 Fifth Avenue
New York, New York 10103

The trademark Yearling® is registered in the U.S. Patent and Trademark Office.

The trademark Dell® is registered in the U.S. Patent and Trademark Office.

ISBN: 0-440-70694-7

Reprinted by arrangement with Franklin Watts, Inc., on behalf of Orchard Books

Printed in the United States of America

September 1991

10 9 8 7 6 5 4 3 2 1

OPM

Contents

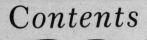

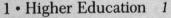

THE BOY
WHO OWNED
THE SCHOOL

1.
Higher
Education

N.

Jacob Freisten stood in the shadow of the dumpster in back of the Reddi-Ralph store across from the high school and studied the front of the school carefully, as if considering buying it. Once his mother had read an article in a magazine about positive reinforcement, and for seven or eight days every morning she would greet him with, "Good morning—and how is the boy who owns the school today?" She thought it would help him get better grades. Jacob winced, remembering it—the boy who owned the school. If she only knew how far off the mark that was. On the other hand, he thought, leaning against the dumpster, it wasn't as bad as the time she read the piece about the all-bran diet. They'd even had to eat bran sprinkled on their meat. Jacob had lost seven pounds.

In.

That was the hardest part about school.

Getting in without being noticed. There it was—he had to not be seen. The thing was, when he was seen, or noticed, or watched, things . . . happened. Ridiculous things. He couldn't explain it even to himself. But if people started to notice him, watch him—or the worst, stare at him—one thing led to another and there was always a disaster. Over the years he had noticed it getting worse and worse, and now he just kept from being seen. It wasn't just that he was shy—it was more the way he was, a way that his everyday life had come to be.

Fact: if you get noticed, bad things happen. Solution: don't get noticed.

There were only four doors, two in the front, big ones that led straight into the main halls where everybody could see you, then one at each end of the old, rectangular building. But both of those doors were the kind that only opened from the inside, and you had to be lucky to hit it just right when somebody you didn't know was opening one and you could slip in. Even then there were two rows of lockers, and that's where the jocks usually took lockers for themselves, and that was the worst of all—if the jocks noticed you. They were like sharks smelling blood if they saw you; one of them would say something, then they would all laugh the hard laugh they had, and another of them would poke or jerk or punch or shoulder-hit you, and it was all over.

Once Jacob had been caught in death row— as he thought of the jock locker area—the wrong way at the wrong time and most of the football team had been there and they had shouldered him from one to the next the entire length of the hall like a sack of potatoes, like seals throwing a ball—except that he figured seals were smarter—and the ball had been him, punched and bruised until the jock at the end had jammed him down into a trash barrel by the door to the girls' toilet.

An awful day, that had been. One he had not forgotten and one he still had not found a way to get even for, because he could not bring himself to think evil enough thoughts. Though he was working on it. He figured hell was made for jocks, and it was simply a matter of letting his thoughts sink low enough for an idea to come. . . .

There was an art to getting in. A definite art. He removed his glasses and wiped them gently with the tail of his T-shirt. With the glasses off he was nearly blind and had to squint so that the freckles on his cheeks—he hated them— seemed to become more dense. He was thin, wiry-thin with faded jeans and a zip-up sweatshirt over his T-shirt and scuffed tennis shoes that felt right when he bought them but were too big now and slopped on his feet.

He had high cheekbones and even, blue eyes that saw everything as a fuzzy cloud without glasses, and he thought, when he wore the glasses and could see himself well and looked in the mirror in the school toilet, that he was probably the ugliest boy in history except for one, who was Darrin Murston, and who looked exactly like a pimple about to come to a head.

Timing was everything.

The buses would unload and the main mob

of kids would go in. At that point everything was confused and moving but still too crowded. Then—just as the main group of kids finished going in and the hall monitors were getting ready to head for the rooms and all the kids were busy with their lockers and nobody was paying any attention to the door—then. Right then.

He waited, watched. The buses unloaded, and kids yelled and joked and moved into the building, and still he waited. The last ones began moving to the doors, and two of the buses started to drive away, and he made his move.

Across the street to the right main front door, in the door looking straight ahead, through the kids still dragging back but not looking at them—with a glazed look he had perfected for just this use, getting in—he went right and down the hall to his locker. Perfect.

They were old lockers, with combination locks that never worked right, but he had come one night with a tube of bicycle lubricant and worked at his lock until it was like a fine watch. Three turns, stop, one turn, stop, one turn and click—open and he had his books for the first class, still without looking up, still without

5

seeing or being seen, and he was gone, down the hallway to his homeroom and the first class of the day, English, where he took the back corner chair and sat with his book open, eyes to the front, ignoring everything and being ignored.

Perfect. Another perfect entrance.

A perfect start for another day of education for Jacob Freisten, he thought, looking at the old map of Europe hanging like a tattered shade, then out the window at a bird that flew past the window.

Jacob Freisten—the boy who owned the school.

2.

The Joys of Home Life

HE never thought of it as home somehow, nor his house. When forced to think of it, to deal with it, he thought, as he did now sitting in English waiting for the squeal of the buzzer to announce class: It's this way where I live.

This way:

His mother and father were normal enough except that they drank a bit too much. Not enough to be alcoholics, and they didn't abuse him, but it was enough so that he didn't really know them except as drinkers. Kind of fuzzy

7

looking. His father did something with mutual funds and was always Doing Business even when he was home, which wasn't often, and sometimes the Business was good and he would be happy and drink, and sometimes the Business was bad and he would be sad and drink.

His mother was Completely, Utterly, Totally Committed to his sister's Career.

That was the problem. His sister. She was seventeen and so beautiful that even Jacob admitted it. Her skin was like soft ivory—seemed almost to glow—on top of which she had a perfect figure and naturally pure blonde hair. She had won every teen beauty contest in the state and region, had walls covered with trophies and ribbons for contests ranging from Miss Cement Mixer to Miss Teen Bicycle Wheel, and was fast on her way to becoming Miss America if her mother had anything to do with it.

She called Jacob Buttwad.

It was not just that she hated him—a fact she readily admitted and told him every chance she got. It was more that she considered him a nuisance—something that got in the way. "Like an insect," she said. "Like a slug. I should have drowned you in the toilet when you were small enough to catch."

They gave her the large upstairs bedroom for her room, with a huge bed and a view of the yard and neighborhood, carpeted with lush shag, and a couch—a couch of her own against one wall—and her own bathroom. A couch.

He got a small, dank room in the basement with a cot and a window high in the wall that looked up at a small square of sky. Kind of like a dungeon cell, he thought. Two walls were painted concrete block, and when the weather was warm the humidity in the room was so high that the tape didn't stick and all his posters fell off.

They gave her a car, a small red sporty car with a snappy look—"For her image," his mother said. "To go with her image"—and kept it supplied with gas and tires. She could come and go anytime she wanted.

He got a bike. With two wheels. And to heck with his image. It was a good enough bike, as bikes went, but it had two wheels, not four like a car, and it was too big for him, so that when he pedaled it he felt like he was falling forward all the time, and that made him try to look up, over the top of his glasses, and he was nearly blind over his glasses, so when he rode his bike he spent a lot of time plowing into things. Which meant he didn't ride it all that much. And he had to pedal it, not drive it, and buy tires for it himself.

They gave her an allowance as big as the budget of some small countries—fifty dollars a week.

He got ten—and had to remind his parents when it was time for that. And if he had wanted school lunch (which he did not) he would have had to pay for it out of the ten.

They gave her new dresses, whole new outfits made of real silk, and special bathing suits to show her off.

He got a pair of socks.

They gave her a "coming out" party, with caterers who made little sandwiches by hand, and live music, and a rented banquet room at the Hillary Inn with punch in a glass bowl.

He got a cake most birthdays from Discount Doug's bakery covered with dancing drunk little elephants made of gushy pink frosting that looked like blown styrofoam.

If she got so much as a stain on her precious skin they called in specialists from New York and spent fortunes consulting still other specialists in Switzerland to make certain it was not a permanent blemish that would require cosmetic surgery to maintain her beauty.

He got braces that hummed when he went through the detector device at the entrance to the public library.

It wasn't that he complained or even felt bad about it anymore. It was just life. And God knew, he thought, as he watched another bird fly past, that they had told him often enough it was a temporary problem—if you considered temporary to mean his whole life so far.

"It's only until we get her launched on her career," his mother had said, sipping a martini while his father read some paper about business being either bad or good and sipped his own. They never drank in gulps. Just sipped. "As soon as we get her off and going we can concentrate on you. . . ."

So they knew of it, and said they were going to do something about it. But Jacob lived in the real world and had to deal with reality.

The reality was that for as long as he could

remember, all of his life to date, his sister had only to frown and she was given the earth, the moon, and the stars, any small or large thing she wanted or even thought she might want, and when newspaper and television and radio people wrote and talked of her they tore themselves apart to find more beautiful names for her.

And he was called Buttwad.

And that, he thought as the buzzer sounded, pretty much summed up the old home life.

3.
Trapped

"JACOB, are you listening?"

Jacob's mind snapped back. He had been thinking of his sister, hoping there would be an earthquake with the epicenter just under the little red car, and visualizing the sudden opening of the very earth to take his problems away . . .

"I said, are you listening?"

The English teacher—Mrs. Hilsak—was looking at him. Worse, far worse, some of the other kids had swiveled to stare at him. Bad, really bad. He was being noticed. Disappear me, he prayed. Disappear me, now, from the eyes of all people in this room.

He nodded. "Sorry . . ."

But it was too late. She had asked twice, and that was too much for him to slide back into the gray world of mystery. He started to reach under the desk and pull himself down, then remembered the boogers and gum stuck under there and drew his hand back.

"Stay a moment after class," Mrs. Hilsak said, pinning him with her eyes, and he saw many of the kids smile at this. Mrs. Hilsak was notorious. If you were told to stay late in her class it was the same as telling you you were going to die.

He nodded again.

She went back to the class, talked for another ten minutes or so about using too many adjectives, and the buzzer sounded.

Everybody filed out, which left Jacob sitting alone in the room.

Mrs. Hilsak stared at him.

He appeared to look back but actually was looking just to the right of her head, a method he had perfected over the years.

"Jacob, I don't know what to do with you."

Talk to my sister, he thought—she knows what to do with me. Exactly. Just give her a toilet.

"You're smart, you could do well but it's like . . . like you aren't here. Don't you want to be in school?"

And that, he thought, is the Big Kazumba—right there. Don't I want to be in school? I would rather be in school than be boiled alive, he thought, barely. He said nothing. Used the perfect non-look.

"The truth is you are close to failing English and I know in my heart you could do very well with it. . . ."

He looked down at his desk. Somebody had scratched a dirty word in the surface. He had seen the same word on the toilet walls, the dumpster in back of Reddi-Ralph, the side of a garbage truck, and his sister's diary before she'd caught him by surprise and hit him with a tennis racket in an almost-perfect backhand that loosened his braces and left his forehead looking like a waffle for three weeks. It was not an adjective. Maybe Mrs. Hilsak would cover it later, in nouns. Or was it a verb? If he'd paid more attention in class he might know that, he thought. . . .

Mrs. Hilsak sighed. "I don't want to fail you."

He looked up, to the right of her head. Waited.

"I will accept extra work. Of any kind. I mean, I'm giving you a chance here, do you understand?"

Jacob nodded.

"Anything you want to turn in. A paper, a speech."

He shuddered. Not a speech. Never a speech. Not even for the earthquake under the red car would he do a speech.

"Better yet—as you know, I am directing the class play this fall. We are doing *The Wizard of Oz*. I will even accept work on the play as extra work for English."

A play, he thought. She wants me in a play? God. That would be worse than a speech. Stand up on a stage in front of two, three million people . . . he felt ill. Weak. What was it he'd had for breakfast? It was there now, waiting to come up. Act. In a play. Right. I could let a car run over my foot, he thought desperately—have to be hospitalized with car-foot.

"All the parts are filled," she said, saving his life. "But we need people to do set work, to help run the special effects, the curtain—you could do that. I'll give you extra credit for that, all right?"

And it was in this way, this simple way, because he was flunking English and Mrs. Hilsak tried to be good to him, that Jacob was given to love, given to understand love and to be in love and in a love story and become the boy who truly owned the school.

But that was later, much later, after many twists of fate, and for now the worst of all possible twists had happened. Mrs. Hilsak let him go with a promise that he would show up for rehearsal that afternoon after school, and he left the room at nearly a dead run—but it was too late, too late.

He was going to be late for gym.

4.

The Horror of Gym Class

JACOB had an uncle named Frank who looked like a spark plug. Narrow at the top and bald, wider at the bottom, and tough as nails. Frank had been in the Navy and stationed in the Philippine Islands. Sometimes when Frank visited and drank martinis with Jacob's dad he talked of a girl in the Philippines, and it was a good story except that Jacob's mother always stopped Frank before it was done, and all Jacob ever heard was up to where the girl poured warm oil . . .

Never past that. Just poured warm oil . . .

It was very frustrating. But during the telling of the story of the girl, one time Frank told of a delicacy they love to eat in the Philippines. It was called a baloot—or that's how it sounded —and ladies went around with baskets of them and sold them for about a quarter. So Jacob asked what a baloot was and wished he hadn't.

Just before a goose egg was ready to hatch, they took it from the mother goose and put it in the hot sun, so the heat killed the baby goose inside the shell. Then they buried the egg in warm sand for weeks, so that inside the shell the little dead baby goose (sometimes they used ducks) rotted and putrefied and got runny in a stringy-lumpy-slimy kind of way, and when it was rotted just exactly enough they took it out of the sand, cracked a little hole in the end of the shell, and sucked the entire contents out and ate it.

"Feathers, beak, feet, guts and all," Frank had said, watching everybody turn green. "I tried it once when I was drunk and got a whole string of it about halfway down my throat when I felt the little head coming through and that was it—I lost her. Never tried it again. That was the night that this young woman took me back into a darkened room and poured warm oil . . ."

"Frank, stop it," Jacob's mother cut in. "The children."

The point was Jacob would rather eat a baloot, every day, than go to gym class.

And to be late to gym, to actually be late for gym was so incredibly terrible that it had only happened once before in his life—in the sixth grade—and he had thought then of just shoving his head in the garbage disposal and ending it.

What made gym so bad, he thought, running down the hall, was everything.

You *had* to go to gym in the first place—which he considered a complete waste—and then you had to cope with the gym teacher. A grownup jock (as Jacob thought of him) named Mr. Rocco, who had a neck bigger than his head and seemed to know only three words:

"Gimme a lap."

It was a command he used on any and every person who did not do exactly as he ordered—in short, everybody. But it came down hardest on Jacob, who was not physical. His arms were thin, and he could do only one warping, twisting, torturing pull-up—he felt like an earth-worm hanging on the bar—when everybody else did ten, and so he took laps. He'd been around the gym so many times he'd worn a groove.

You had to go to gym, and then you had to go into the locker room and change into shorts and a T-shirt with everybody else, and some-body always wetted the end of a towel and snapped you with it—fun for everybody but the snappee, usually Jacob, who found himself driven into the lockers when he got hit.

Fun. Gym, he thought, rounding the corner by the locker room, was such fun. About as much fun as having a sister who was a beauty queen.

Too late.

He was too late. Everybody had changed and was already out on the gym floor playing volley-ball and jumping around on the mats. That meant he would have to change and come into the gym alone, not at the back of the group, and everybody would turn and stare at him. Notice him.

Arrggh!

In gym shorts that were so big he could tie

the waist around his neck, in a T-shirt that prac-
tically hung to the floor, the earthworm would
have to enter the gym alone, the center of attention.

Madness.

Maybe he could be sick. If he stuck his finger
down his throat and puked he could tell the
gym teacher he was sick. He *was* sick. Sick of
gym. No, that wouldn't work—Rocco would
just tell him to run until he died.

Maybe that was the answer. He could just
die. No. He thought about the other half of the
idea: He could run.

There was the answer. He could just enter
the gym and start running, enter running and
move right into doing laps because Rocco would
just have him doing laps anyway. Maybe everybody wouldn't stare at him.

Yeah.

He changed quickly, threw his clothes in the
locker, tied his shoes, and ran for the gym door,
slammed his shoulder into it and hit the floor
of the gym running at a full lope.

Right up the middle of Maria Tresser's back.

5.
Hit and Run

It was definitely not a good start for gym class.

Maria Tresser was the most beautiful, the most popular, the most everything girl in school. She had it all. She was scheduled to play the Wicked Witch in *The Wizard of Oz*, because she was so good as an actress and the role was so hard to do right. She had a dazzling smile. She did not wear braces and never needed them, did not wear glasses and never needed them, had full, beautiful, black hair that hung down in soft waves. And to top it all was nice, truly nice, and everybody loved her.

Jacob went over her like a truck.

He knocked her down, and his momentum was so strong that he couldn't stop. He actually put a foot in the middle of her back and ran over her, kept running two more steps before he realized what had happened and tried to stop and go back to help her. Had he not been going so fast it might have worked, but as it was his feet stopped and the rest of him kept going. He went down like he'd been hit from behind, flopping end over end on the gym floor like a beached carp, and each time he flipped all he could think was: I wish I was dead, I wish I was dead, I wish I was dead.

Not really his best start for a gym class.

He scrambled to his feet and ran back to where Maria was just getting up. "I'm sorry. I was late and I thought if I ran . . ."

"No problem." Maria dusted off her shorts, tucked her T-shirt back in where it had come out, rubbed the end of her nose where it had slammed into the floor, ran a hand through her hair, and started to trot back to the volleyball game. "I shouldn't have been playing in the fast lane—my fault."

Jacob's heart went out to her. What absolute class! It was like nothing had happened, she just bounced up. Then he looked around. The entire gym had stopped. Everybody had turned from what they were doing, and they were staring at him, through him, into him.

"Heck of a way to get a girl," somebody said. "Running over her."

"Hit and run . . ." somebody else laughed.

And Rocco turned from where he had been tightening the volleyball net. His eyes like fiery little marbles, his neck swollen, his shoulders curved forward like some primitive beast, he stood and looked at Jacob, and his mouth opened and he said, "Gimme a lap."

Jacob started trotting in the endless circle around the gym, eyes glazed, staring down at the wooden floor, his brain turning to liquid. All of them were staring at him. All around the gym. He could feel their eyes on him like a hot wave, watching him as he trotted. The earthworm in his too-big shorts and T-shirt, wimping around the gym.

25

It felt like a year, two years, before they started playing volleyball and jumping on the mats again, a year or two while he trotted around the gym in a circle like a trained pony, wishing the floor would open and swallow him, but it was probably eight or nine laps, and then he settled down to the normal torture of just running. When Rocco said, "Gimme a lap," he didn't mean just a lap. He meant the victim to keep running until he said to stop running. The problem was that Jacob figured Rocco's attention span and memory were something on the order of a paramecium's, so when he told Jacob to take a lap he promptly forgot him, and often Jacob would run the whole gym period.

Running, even all period, was preferable to the other choices—volleyball, for instance. In volleyball he simply became a target for anybody who wanted to spike the ball, and the few times he had tried to "play" volleyball he had spent the whole game trying to look like he was playing but really running in little circles trying to get out of the line of fire—which never worked. The spiked ball invariably nailed him in the top of the head, driving his eyes lower than his glasses, and of course that meant he tripped over everybody else and turned the game into a shambles—which triggered Rocco who then made him run laps.

A vicious circle. Like the circle around the gym.

But even volleyball was preferable to gymnastics. Jacob had blocked the memory of the only time Rocco had insisted on him doing gymnastics—the vault and the rings—but the misery was still there. On the vault he had jumped off the board and missed the horse entirely, probably because his legs were so strong from all the running. He came down on his face on the mat eight feet past the horse with a mighty splatting sound—there was still a stain on the mat where he hit. On the rings he found his left arm was weaker than his right, so that he hung like a chicken with a broken wing, just hung there while Rocco yelled and grunted at him. . . .

Past halfway through the period and Jacob had hit his stride, an easy trot he could probably do all day. I could probably run down antelope in Africa with this trot, he thought, probably lope around the world, Rocco yelling at me—

just floating along, when he felt his right tennis shoe coming untied.

Problem. A bad problem. Rocco might have forgotten he was running, might have even forgotten who he was, but Rocco knew when anyone stopped running. Even to tie their shoes. He could sense a stopped runner by the change of rhythm in the air currents. People who stopped running designated laps for any reason short of actual, proven death were in for trouble with Rocco, who used his other sentence on them:

"Gimme more laps."

This usually meant you were supposed to run laps until you were thirty or thirty-five years old, but worse, far worse, if Jacob stopped to tie his shoes and Rocco hit him with his second sentence, he would be the focus of the class again. They'd all stop and stare at him: the earthworm standing there while Rocco yelled at him.

Jacob stole a quick look. The lace was completely loose now, trailing about a foot in back and to the inside of the shoe. But the old caged clock on the wall was moving as well. Only six minutes left before Rocco would release them to the locker room.

Six minutes.

If he ran by swinging his right foot out in a small circle, it would swing the lace out and he wouldn't step on it with his left foot. He tried it and it worked, but it made him run funny, his feet going whummmmmp-whump, whummmmmp-whump, like somebody with one leg about a foot longer than the other.

Four minutes.

Whummmmmmp-whump.

And he would have made it except that with three minutes to go he felt somebody looking at him, staring at him, and out of the corner of his eye saw with shock that Maria Tresser had stopped playing and had turned and was watching him run.

Whummmmmmp-whump.

Staring right at him.

The thought was enough to make him forget to swing his right foot out.

His left foot came down on the lace and stopped his right foot just as it started to move forward.

For a brief part of a second there was a mad flurry of shoes slapping the floor as he tried to stay up but it was no use. He knew it was no use. He was supposed to fall. That's what he thought: I am supposed to fall. All my life I have been living just so I can do this now, step on my shoelace and fall while Maria Tresser is staring at me.

He went down like an oak.

In front of the coach's table used for basketball games was a wastebasket full of styrofoam cups from the game the night before. Some of them still had pop in them. It tasted like Coke. Jacob came down on top of the wastebasket, which tipped, and he slid into the cups on his face while the wastebasket went spinning out ahead of him across the gym floor, just as the early buzzer sounded ending the gym period.

Another gym class completed, he thought—perfect.

6.

The Lure of the Stage

E had also developed moving through the hallways to an art form. From gym he had to go to industrial arts. He changed in a darkened corner of the locker room which smelled of foot powder and fungus at the same time—a corner everybody else avoided, which they called the Rat Corner—and moved into the halls.

First he headed to his locker to get his letter holder. They had to make plastic letter holders in shop, which seemed insane—how many fifteen-year olds needed letter holders? Jacob got about one letter a year, and two cards from his aunt who traveled all over the world and kept writing him things like: "Nepal is great," or "Brazil is great," or "Paris is great." He didn't need the letter holder about as much as he didn't need to do *The Wizard of Oz* but he liked shop more than the rest of school. It was dumb, but Mr. Stans who taught the class didn't bother him except to come around the room once or twice and pretend to look at his work. He didn't really hassle anybody since he spent all his time making an endless row of gun racks, which he gave to relatives for Christmas. Jacob figured he must have the best armed family in the world. Figure ten, twelve gun racks, each one holding five guns—fifty, sixty guns. The Stans family must be like an army.

It was knowing the flow of traffic in the halls that was the secret. The classes were staggered so that three bells rang for the end of each period, to avoid major jams in the halls. Just as the first bell segment kids were hitting their classrooms, the bell for the second one started, and when that finished the third triggered.

It should have worked, but of course it was madness. The first one ran into the second, and they both got tangled with the third, and the end result was pandemonium—a traffic jam worse than pictures Jacob had seen of people trying to drive into Los Angeles. Gridlock. Kids jammed in the corners, fighting to get to their lockers, elbowing each other, trying to run, while the hall monitors—Rocco with his neck swollen—screamed at them to slow down to a walk.

But in this chaos Jacob had discovered a pulse, a rhythm of sanity. Just between the first two bell segments there would be a ripple in which it was possible to move without too much effort, a kind of peaceful line that moved along, and he knew exactly when it went past the gym, his locker, and then on to the industrial arts room.

He grabbed the ripple like a salmon heading upstream, followed it to his locker, picked up his letter holder and moved along—looking down, just letting it take him—until it came to room 302, industrial arts. There he peeled off, took the corner bench in the back of the room, and started to sand.

Mr. Stans used the belt sander for all his gun racks. But he made the kids sand everything

by hand. The result was that all their letter holders looked like garbage, rounded ends and
scratches and crude smudges, while his gun
racks looked polished and clean and professional. He was always pointing his handiwork
out to the kids like the class was some kind of
competition. "See how clean the edges are?"
he'd say, holding up a gun rack. "You have to
make yours the same. It's just elbow grease."

Jacob figured Stans did that because he had
a problem with self worth. Jacob understood
that.

I wish I had a belt sander for my life, he
thought, rubbing the letter holder but thinking
of the coming rehearsal.

He didn't dread it much more than, say, having his braces "tuned," which he didn't have to
do anymore but which used to make him feel
like his head was coming apart. Back when he
wore braces his orthodontist would take the little chisel and hammer and pliers and just about
rip his head open, laughing and talking about
basketball all the while. He thought all boys
liked basketball. Then at Christmas he would
send Jacob a card covered with little elves and

bunnies telling him to be a "good little boy" and "brush and floss regularly."

There it is, Jacob thought, sanding—I can keep the old cards from my orthodontist in my letter holder.

Funny how things work out.

"Good work, good work." Stans came up in back of him. "Make the edges a little neater. Check that gun rack over there and you'll see what I mean. Clean edges, smooth . . ."

After industrial arts was lunch, then study period, math, social science, and rehearsal.

Rehearsal.

And the day had started so well, too. He had gotten in so smoothly, gotten past the jocks, moved well in the halls, even into the seat in English. Everything was working just right until Mrs. Hilsak nailed him.

Rehearsal.

Even if he just worked on the sets he'd have to be with the others. He'd be noticed. They'd start to watch him, and he'd goof up because they were watching him, and it would all snowball into a disaster. He could ruin the play. Easily. Just by being there.

Mrs. Hilsak should know that. He should get extra credit for *not* being involved with the play.

That was it. He'd explain things to her, and maybe she would understand and let him off.

His best possible contribution to the theater, he thought—stay away from it. It was the only safe thing to do. That's how he'd tell her.

Of course then he'd have to talk to her.

Hmmmm.

He sanded on the letter holder, making more smudges and lines and rounding the corners still more. He looked up at the clock. Twenty more minutes to lunch. Twenty minutes to stand at the bench and sand.

He might as well let the daydream come.

7.

Lost in Fantasia

THE dreams were a continuing battle. For a time Jacob had had one friend, a boy named Clayton—before Clayton's father either got fired or promoted and was either forced to move or wanted to move, depending on how Clayton was feeling when he told the story. Clayton had been Jacob's only friend and wasn't much of a friend at that, because he went to a different school and Jacob had only seen him once or twice a week for about three months before he moved. But Clayton was the best friend Jacob had, and once he had told Jacob he was weird because he daydreamed in color, and the dreams were stories, and Jacob had no control over them.

Jacob hadn't known it was strange until Clayton said so, just thought he had bad dream-luck, and wasn't sure exactly how it was strange, since Clayton had been kind of weird himself. He had collected dead ants, collected them and kept them in a jar. He didn't kill them, just kept the ones he found that were already dead. Jacob wasn't sure somebody who was always looking for dead ants was a good judge of other people's weirdness.

But the dreams were strange. They were in color and were whole stories, with beginnings, middles, and ends, and the true problem was that he really couldn't control them.

Oh, he could start them like anybody. Just let his eyes glaze over and stick in an idea and there it would go. Like today. He wanted to dream about Maria Tresser, which was a normal dream for him, and wanted to make the dream be about maybe him and Maria being together, and so he started this dream as if he weren't like he was, weren't an absolutely perfect example of a geek, but was somebody normal with a pretty good car and an ugly sister, and he never tripped and was, really, quite good at whatever he chose to do.

That's what he started.

And the idea was that in the daydream, in the twenty minutes left in shop, he would get Maria to go out on a date with him, perhaps to a movie, and he would drive well and not wreck the car, and after the movie maybe they would go someplace and park, and he would turn to her and she would be beautiful sitting there in the car seat with the curves of her hair falling in the moonlight, and she would ask about his poor, ugly sister, and he would reach out and touch her hair. . . .

And that's as far as it got. That's how he wanted the dream to go. But he had to be careful, and this time he'd forgotten to be cautious. He had just turned the dream loose, and the last time he'd done that was when he daydreamed he was a test pilot testing a new fighter while Maria Tresser watched, and at the last moment he couldn't remember if he was supposed to pull the stick back or push it forward to climb, and he had flown into a mountain at about eighteen hundred miles an hour just as the math teacher asked him for the answer to a problem.

Still, this time he thought he was safe. No planes, no guns—nothing that could blow up. No sharp objects. He even daydreamed the car had an automatic transmission, because he wasn't sure if his shifting was smooth enough.

His mistake was that he overdressed. In the daydream he had shoulders, real shoulders, and a kind of a loose fitting jacket. He looked fairly cool and could have left it that way, but he thought a tie would make him look even better.

That was the mistake.

He included a tie, loose at the neck, dark blue with small white spots. It made the outfit, just made it. Not too loud, not crazy—just right. But a tie, still, a tie tied around his neck.

His neck.

He should have known better.

The dream started at his locker. He would be just turning from his locker, and Maria would be coming down the hall, and she would smile at him and wave, and he would ask her for a date, and she would say, sure, she'd love it, and then it would jump to the evening and they would be parked. But it would start at his locker. That was the plan.

He looked at the clock. Still fifteen minutes to go. Easy. Three minutes to set it up, four more minutes of chit-chat and he'd be in the car with her.

He glazed his eyes and there it was.

The hallway, some kids moving by, Maria coming toward him, her hair bouncing. She waved first (a nice twist). He had one hand on his locker door, which was open. He threw a book in the mess at the bottom, turned casually to return the wave—it was the only courteous thing to do—and as he turned he slammed the locker door.

Unfortunately, as he wheeled the tie flew out a bit, and when he slammed the locker shut the tie got caught in the door. Things blew up fast after that. He reached to pull at the tie, but it was caught tight. He raised one foot to brace it against the locker, but the other foot slipped from beneath him and he went down, wheeling as he went so his back was to the locker and his feet out in front of him, hanging on his tie like a mini-gallows, his eyes starting to bulge.

Two students tripped on his outflung legs, falling loudly. They in turn tripped more students, and soon the hallway was a panic of students going down over each other, falling and sliding.

He had one fleeting picture of Maria with a hand to her mouth, staring at him—then he had to fight for his very life, jerking and wheeling and pulling at the tie, trying to get his legs under him to stand, trying to reach back up over his head and open the door, clawing, fighting, scrabbling for life, everything going red, then black, his life fading. . . .

The bell rang. Shop was over.

He looked in his hands at the letter holder. He'd rubbed so hard he'd broken it.

He started for the hall. No ties. He'd have to remember that in the future.

No daydreams with ties in them.

8.

Life Beneath
the Boards

THE auditorium was a horrifying mass of people running every which way, yelling, pointing. At one side Maria Tresser stood, waiting for instructions, one hand on her hip and the other running through her hair. There were probably three people for every one who would be in the play—Mrs. Hilsak's plays were always popular and many tried out for them—plus a whole bunch of smaller kids from the elementary school down the block. The littler kids didn't make any sense until Jacob remembered the movie of *The Wizard of Oz*—all the little Munchkins and monsters. That must be what they were for, the small ones.

Mrs. Hilsak was in the center of the stage, holding a clipboard, directing the madness.

Jacob was in a strange mood. Normally he would be home now, hiding in the basement, working his way through the refrigerator, or trying to find a way to torment his sister—he thought of it as getting even—and his mind was not in a school frame. For that reason he went too far into the auditorium. He meant to stop in back, up under the balcony where it was partially darkened and he might not be seen. He thought if he could remain out of sight Mrs. Hilsak might not notice him, and he could stay a few moments and then drift out, go home and start digging a pit with sharpened stakes in the front yard to catch his sister—he figured he could bait it with a couple of glamor magazines and she'd walk right in.

But he went too far, got caught in the light, and Mrs. Hilsak saw him.

"Jacob, come up here please."

And of course he had to go. Down the aisle between the seats, across the front, everybody looking at him, even the Munchkins, to the left of the stage where there were three steps up. He started up them, saw that Maria had turned slightly and was watching him, felt his face go red, forgot to watch the steps, and tripped on the top one.

He arrived on the stage face down, his glasses driven halfway through his head.

Perfect.

He stood, brushed his pants, straightened his glasses, and waited, looking but not looking at Mrs. Hilsak, not even looking but not looking at Maria.

"I want you to be in charge of the fog machine," Mrs. Hilsak said. "Come with me and I'll show you what to do. Maria, you come as well, since it concerns you the most."

She turned and walked off the stage to the left, Maria following and Jacob bringing up the rear.

This is bad, he thought. We're going to be doing something together. Not even a daydream this time. For real. I'm dead. One sharp object and I'm dead. Thank God I'm not wearing a tie. This is bad. Deadly. What is a fog machine?

I'm going to be doing something with Maria involving a fog machine?

Please Lord, don't let it be nuclear.

Mrs. Hilsak led them down a small stairway, around a bend and through a dusty hallway, and into a low doorway which required them to crouch.

They were beneath the stage. Overhead they could hear the muffled thud and rumble of people moving. There was not quite room to stand beneath the stringers that held the stage floor up—they had to hunch over as Mrs. Hilsak led them to a point beneath the center of the stage. On a small platform was a gray device, a machine with three lights and a handle like a pump handle on the top. There was a filler cap near that and a bottle of some kind of pale green chemical sitting on the floor next to the machine. A wire ran to a plug over on the wall. Out the front of the machine stuck a funnel-like pipe, and almost straight above the machine was a trapdoor cut into the stage floor. A sliding bolt held the trapdoor in place, with a handle that stuck down so it could be pushed open and the trapdoor allowed to swing open.

This could be from another planet, Jacob thought, watching the machine warily. A cyborg. It could take over the world.

"This is the fog machine," Mrs. Hilsak said. "It's really quite simple. You pour this chemical into the filler spout, pump the pressure up with the pump handle, hit this switch, and when the green light comes on you hit the next switch, this one, and the machine will begin to emit fog. Of course you want the trapdoor open when it happens, otherwise the whole place will fill up with fog and you won't be able to see what you're doing. I had the janitor grease the bolt on the trapdoor so it will work easily." She paused. "Any questions so far?"

Jacob said nothing. Maria shook her head.

"Now, timing is everything. You have to work this out together, and it's critical, the critical part of the whole play. At the point when Dorothy throws the water on the Wicked Witch to melt her, the trapdoor has to open and the fog flow up so that Maria—the Wicked Witch—can lower herself down into the opening and appear to melt."

Timing, Jacob thought. Critical. Melt. I'm going to melt Maria.

"I'll leave you two to work out the exact timing of it. . . ." And she turned and left them alone.

Alone, Jacob thought, at last, looking but not looking at Maria—I'm alone with the woman I'm supposed to melt. He licked his lips, which were strangely dry. I should speak, he thought, I should say something. Nothing came. He moved a bit until he was beneath the trapdoor. Took a deep breath. Let it out.

"Well," Maria said finally. "We're going to work together."

Jacob looked but didn't look at her. Shrugged.

"You know, I see you in the halls and I see you in the classrooms but it's like I'm not seeing you. Why is that?" She smiled. Even, white teeth, of course.

Because I'm a geek, he thought, and you can't see geeks.

"I mean the first time I ever got a chance to speak to you is when you ran over me in gym today. How can that be? In one school, how can it be possible to never really see somebody?"

She's actually talking to me. For part of a second he looked at her, really looked at her, and froze. She was looking right into his eyes. Seeing him, noticing him, talking to him.

To Jacob.

He turned away, a bit too fast, started to lose

his balance and raised a hand to grab at the ceiling to keep from falling. He missed the stringers and accidentally grabbed the bolt that held the trapdoor in place. It slid easily, popped back, and the trapdoor dropped open.

Two Munchkins, boys in the third grade from Grandview Elementary, had been standing on the trapdoor. They were already nervous and frightened with all the activity on the stage, were working very hard at holding their positions and not doing anything wrong, when the bottom suddenly dropped out of their world.

They plummeted down, landing on Jacob, sure they were going to be eaten by the Big Wizard, and immediately started screaming and scratching, trying to get away from him, who wanted nothing more than to get them away.

Jacob had one quick picture of Maria starting to double over, laughing, then the two Munchkins ran across his face and he didn't see anything.

And it wasn't even a daydream.

9.

Phantom of the Auditorium

NOW he couldn't talk to her. No matter what.

After the disaster beneath the stage when she had laughed and had actually asked him, personally, about why she never saw him—after all that he could not talk to her.

What made it difficult, maybe impossible, was that he still had to run the fog machine and be part of the play or he would flunk English. If he flunked English, or even got an F in English for one report card period but still managed to pass it—just that F meant that he would get noticed the wrong way by his parents.

Normally they worked on his sister and tried to make her even more beautiful and more or less forgot he was there. But if he pulled a bad grade he would get the serious lectures from his parents. That's when they would sit him down and ask him if he were:

Doing drugs.

Contemplating teen suicide.

Having difficulty with his peers.

Feeling depressed.

Having adjustment problems.

Feeling inadequate.

Feeling unmotivated.

Feeling overmotivated.

Feeling bad about himself.

Not feeling anything—that is, not being in touch with his feelings.

Depending on what his mother had been reading lately and discussing with his father or if he told them the truth, that it was all of the above except drugs, they'd just ignore the answer and go on until they were satisfied they had Straightened Him Up.

So he had to stay and work the fog machine or get an F and go through the serious lectures at home.

But he couldn't face Maria Tresser again. As long as he lived and maybe a bit longer.

So it was a difficult situation.

Days passed, and he had to be at rehearsal every afternoon. He evolved a plan that seemed to work out. He would hide up in the darkened corner of the auditorium until they were well into rehearsal and just getting to the part in the second act when Maria had to disappear as the Wicked Witch, and at that point he would sneak into the space beneath the stage. Then when it came time to open the trapdoor he would let it drop and move away, so he was out of sight. The first time Maria lowered to her knees and looked down inside.

"Jacob?"

But he was back around a brace, hidden in a corner, and after a moment she shrugged upside down.

"I don't understand—he was here a minute ago," she said to someone back on top. "I just wanted to tell him to lower the trapdoor a little sooner, when I start my death scream. . . ."

When rehearsals were over he moved out the back door of the space beneath the stage, out a back exit of the auditorium which opened into an alley, and down the alley toward home.

By the third night the plan was working smoothly. They didn't expect to see him, and Maria had quit looking or calling to him. He was there but not there, the phantom beneath the stage—he actually heard one of the Munchkins asking somebody what was opening and closing the trapdoor. Not who, but what.

Sometimes he would move around, tripping and bumping his head on the stringers and formers that held the stage up, trying to follow where Maria was on the floor above by her voice, and think, There she is, just there, right above me on this spot, only inches away. He would close his eyes and think of her, her hair falling on her shoulders, her eyes when she had looked at him, straight and clear and direct, when he looked but didn't look at her.

Right there, above his head.

And he knew then that he loved her, loved her more than anything, loved her more than he hated the idea of baloots, and he also knew that it would never come to anything, that he would always be beneath the stage and she would always be on top, because that's the way things were. Some people were above-stage people, some people lived beneath the stage.

A terrible sadness took him then and he even forgot to trip on the fog machine and spent nearly a whole rehearsal without tripping or falling or banging his head against the stringers.

The hallways and classrooms were worse.

If Maria had given up trying to speak to him during rehearsals, she had not given up in the halls or classrooms. Twice she cornered him just before English and he would have had to say something, except that he'd suddenly ducked out as if he had to go to the bathroom.

Maximum embarrassment with minimum effort, he thought, staggering to the door rather than speak to the most beautiful girl in school, a girl he loved more than he hated baloots.

But it worked.

The only other class he had with her was gym, and that wasn't a problem because she played volleyball and Rocco had him doing laps for presumably the rest of his life.

Hallways proved to be more dangerous.

He was moving with a ripple from English to gym, just passing the jock area, when he saw Maria coming toward him. She had seen him and obviously wanted to say something. The only way to escape was to move out of the ripple and into the next wave of students. He looked over his shoulder and made his move, picking up speed to a trot.

But he didn't look straight ahead and he ran smack into Bee-Bee Wainright. It was like hitting a living wall.

Bee-Bee was the center on the football team and cordially hated anybody who did not play football, including, probably, his mother. It was rumored that his nickname had something to do with brain size and that they were going to start a special class to help him learn to speak human—and while Jacob doubted both of these rumors he knew it was wrong to run into Bee-Bee. Very wrong.

Bee-Bee grabbed him by the neck as if somebody had given him an early Christmas present, and managed to fit Jacob almost completely inside Mary Jo Callis's locker, though Mary Jo had the bottom filled with books, an old winter coat, her cheerleading pom-poms, and what was apparently an antique peanut-butter-and-jelly sandwich, judging by smell.

Jacob found his legs, both arms, and his glasses and removed himself from the locker carefully, like untangling spaghetti. He wanted to apologize to Mary Jo for crushing her pom-poms but moved off down the hallway when he saw she was laughing at him.

Love, he thought, watching Maria's back disappear in the crowd—love can be cruel.

10.
Misery

IT was possible that his heart was broken.

He wasn't sure because he'd never had a broken heart before except for the time when he almost got a puppy and was given a chance to hold it and pet it and then didn't get it and always thought that might be the same, sort of, as having had a puppy and losing it. He felt bad then. That might have been close to a broken heart, but it had happened when he was young, before he discovered love, and this was different.

It was very possible that he had a broken heart.

He thought of it often. The awful, gray-ugly, right-down, terrible, tearing agony of it stayed with him all the time but seemed to be worse when something else was going wrong. It was like having a bad toothache while somebody put your finger on a rock and hit it with a hammer. The pain in the finger didn't really make the toothache worse but it sure didn't help, either.

In the mornings he came up from his room to get a bowl of cereal and had to face the normal things: his sister sitting at the table looking as if she'd been sculpted, every hair in place, not a freckle or mole or mark, her eyes blank as a bored snake, daintily eating a grapefruit and one piece of dry toast, looking at him with open disgust and turning away while he dumped Froot Loops in a bowl and covered them with milk and crunched himself awake.

Then, right then, it was worse.

Or while resticking all his posters to the walls in the basement, which he did every other day or so when they fell down because of the humidity, and which only helped to remind him that he lived beneath the house the same way he lived beneath the stage that held Maria; beneath the house where his sister had a room, car, couch, stereo, and he had concrete-block walls painted maroon and a throw rug and square boxes for furniture and a small clock-radio, the same way he was beneath the stage where all of what he wanted was above him.

Then, right then, it was even worse.

Or the way it made his judgment wrong and caused him to make mistakes he never would have made otherwise—like coming home from school two blocks over, the wrong way, completely forgetting about the maniac who lived on the corner of Hennessy who had a loose dog that was part pit bull and part alligator. Without thinking, Jacob had walked—not run but actually walked with his head in a gray funk—past the man's yard. The dog had come over the low fence like a mouth on a cannon shell and nearly got him, and he'd spent the better part of an hour sitting on the low limb of an elm tree watching the dog froth and chew at the bark around the base until a cat crossed the street half a block down. The cat made it to a power pole with two-and-a-half inches to spare but it gave Jacob time to get away.

Then it was worse still.

Or at night when he listened to music on his clock-radio and he would close his eyes and remember how Maria's hair fell in gentle folds and was soft around her temples or how the line of her neck went curving down to her shoulders just so, lie there thinking about Maria and how he would never be able to really talk to her, never be able to tell her how he felt, because when he saw her, just saw her, his tongue stuck so hard to the roof of his mouth that it would take a crowbar to get it loose, and he couldn't even look at her without looking at her any longer but now could only not look at her.

Then it was the very worst.

His life became a roaring agony of mistakes and disasters even more terrible than usual.

He forgot his rule about coming in the side door of school and was passed down the jock locker row again, end over end, and jammed into the trash container by the girls' bathroom, which he decided was a very bad trash container to be jammed into, even worse than Mary Jo Callis's locker.

Another day he went right in the front door of school without timing it, and several kids said hi to him, which startled him so much he mistakenly got caught in the stream of kids going to the downstairs row of lockers, and it took him fifteen minutes to get all the way around and back to his locker.

Which made him late for algebra.

Which made him get noticed.

Mr. Hankenton called him up to the front of the room to work out a problem on the board, up in front of all the kids, or as he thought of it, UP IN FRONT OF ALL THE KIDS, and Jacob was stunned, completely numb-stunned, to find that his feet carried him up there—like traitors—carried him against his will to the front and that his brain worked the problem correctly and his hands wrote the numbers and letters correctly, also against his will, and he watched in horror as his body and legs and brain all went against him and worked everything right and turned him—hating it—turned him to face the class while Mr. Hankenton complimented him. All he could think was how he hated his legs and brain and hands for getting him into such a predicament, and he tried to look over the class at the wall as he made his way back to the seat, tried to look over them and figure out how in the world he had come to know algebra. How could being in love and having a broken heart make him know algebra?

Misery.

Worse, far worse, in his funk he forgot to hide in back of the dumpster by the Reddi-Ralph before school one morning, walked right out in the open and started up the steps, and somebody waved at him, and he waved back.

He waved back.

He didn't even know who waved, didn't even know he waved back.

He was losing it.

It was possible that he had a broken heart.

11.

Tomorrow

MRS. Hilsak found him just before dress rehearsal. She nearly had to tackle him. He was in the back corner beneath the stage and thought it was Maria looking for him. He moved into the shadows to get away but she saw him and stopped him before he could make the door.

"Jacob, what's the matter with you?" Mrs. Hilsak had to crouch beneath the stage.

He said nothing, looked to her side, ached.

"You just . . . disappear. We look for you but you just vanish. Can I help you?"

You could tell Maria I am dying inside, he thought — tell her that the alligator-pitbull of love has my heart. Tell her I am eating myself up. Tell her that I even waved at somebody and can now work algebra against my will.

He said nothing.

"Well. I just want to make sure you understand. We don't use the fog machine until the first performance tomorrow night. Tonight during dress rehearsal you just pretend. All right?"

He sort of nodded and she left.

Pretend, he thought. It's all pretend.

The dress rehearsal began perfectly.

The play went on above and he went on below, waiting. When he heard her death scream start he pretended to turn on the fog machine, opened the trap door and disappeared out the door before Maria could let herself down the hole. Just like all the other rehearsals.

He walked home in the dark where he went to his room in the basement and listened to music until his eyes closed and he slept.

He had a dream about Maria. She was walking down a street, and a bulldog jumped over a fence at her, and he rushed to save her and would have done all right, except that the bulldog turned into his sister, turned on him and dumped a bowl of Froot Loops on his head.

He awakened in a sweat, spitting imaginary Froot Loops out of his mouth, and sat awake in his darkened room listening to the posters falling because it was the second day and thought he couldn't go on this way. Something would get him if he didn't straighten out. Either the dog would rip him apart or the jocks would set him up for permanent housekeeping in a garbage can or his sister would bury him in Froot Loops or he would turn into a professional mathematician.

Something would get him.

He had to take charge of this thing. Get back to normal.

Tomorrow.

He closed his eyes. A poster fell. He turned the clock radio off and let sleep take him.

Have to straighten this out, he thought, the sleep coming down. Tomorrow. Straighten this out tomorrow.

12.
Surrender

IN.

That was it. That was the hard part. He stood by the Reddi-Ralph dumpster and studied the front of the school, waiting.

Timing was everything.

He had to catch that exact moment when it was right to enter, when he could slide in between groups of students and not be noticed.

Work carefully to his locker and then to English and get into his desk and sit, there but not there, the phantom student, the boy who owned the school.

It was simple, really. Nothing had changed. He'd had a bad week, but in the light of morning he knew it for what it was—a mistake. A dream. Another dream gone wrong. He couldn't love Maria. Not really. No more than a snail could love a princess—there was physics involved. It was like making up be down. An impossibility. Geeks didn't get to love Maria. And when he knew that he also knew that everything else would fall into place. Everything would be back to normal.

He had the play to do. But he could just run the fog machine for two nights, turn it on and get out and everything would be all right.

In.

Timing was everything.

He moved through the doors, down the hall, got his books, and was into the room.

Maria was there, in the front, and he felt her eyes on him, but he was in control now, tight control, and he looked past her, past everything, at the wall.

Mrs. Hilsak said nothing to him, went right into verbs, and he went back to thinking about normal things: How to get even with his sister. A way to get the posters to stick to the walls.

How to get his sister's diary and use it to negotiate. . . . Maybe he couldn't have an upstairs room but perhaps if he worked it right he could at least hang his posters in her room and then just come up and look at them once in a while. If he had her diary he could work a deal like that, maybe even sit on her couch and look at them.

And he didn't daydream either. Everything safe and sound. None of those fantasies or silly hopes. He had it now, knew where it was going.

At the end of class he was gone, clean and gone and into the ripple movement before anybody could talk to him. After that it was just getting through the day, one class to the next. He didn't get called on once, not even in math, and until lunch he was sure he had it worked out right.

Then the glitches started. During lunch it came, the first indication that things weren't going to stay normal, and that love had ruined his life forever.

It began in the cafeteria line. They were having pizza (only of course it wasn't pizza but what they called pizza—the only pizza Jacob had ever seen that he could drink), and he never took the pizza. He wouldn't make his *sister* eat the pizza. This time he was looking toward the front of the line where oddly enough Maria was standing, and he nodded, and the lady put the pizza on his tray.

Rocco was in charge of the cafeteria.

If it hit your tray, you ate it. That was Rocco's rule. And if it hit your tray and you ate it, you ate it all. He watched everybody like a hawk and that meant Jacob of course had to eat the pizza.

Drink the pizza.

All of it.

Plus, on the pizza order they gave him a piece of bread that had been backed over by a garlic truck, and after he drank the pizza and ate the bread, Jacob had breath that could be cut into chunks.

He sat alone at the end of a long table, finished eating, and tried to hold his breath.

Nothing helped. He could hold it for half a minute as he walked out and down the hall, but then he had to let it out, and it was worse when it came out in bursts. Kids around him almost dropped.

All because he had looked at Maria.

The rest of the afternoon was spent in a green haze, trying to hold his breath for an hour at a stretch, letting it blast out, getting sick from the smell. He felt his control slipping.

Classes changed. Crawled.

In the middle of the last class, social studies, he began to worry about the play.

It started slowly.

He thought first of the Munchkins. They were unpredictable. Little kids running around all over on top of the stage. If they got their positions wrong . . .

Then the worry grew. If one Munchkin was out of place, standing on the trapdoor, and Maria couldn't get into the right place, and he pulled the lever . . . or what if the lever jammed and the trapdoor didn't open or the fog machine didn't work or . . .

By the end of the school day he was in a nervous froth. He went home to eat dinner and found to his horror that his mother had heard about the play. The news was dropped on him at the table like an anvil. They were having some kind of chunky yogurt casserole because it was supposed to be good for his sister's com-

70

plexion, and Jacob was trying to chew it, though he knew the smell had mixed with the garlic and pizza and made his breath glow in the dark, and his mother said:

"I hear you're in a play tonight, Jacob. Is that right?"

"What?" His sister stopped with a spoonful halfway to her mouth. "You're in a play? What play? *The Hunchback of Notre Dame?*"

"It's *The Wizard of Oz*," Jacob said, "and I'm not in it. I work on the sets, that's all."

"Still," his mother said. "I think we should go. It's your first time, your debut in the theater—I think we'll come. I'll call your father and tell him to hurry home."

His father was working late.

"We'll make a night of it, shall we?" His mother turned to his sister. "You can come too."

"Mother."

"I insist."

"But really, Mother. *The Wizard of Oz*. All those geeky little people running around in this geeky little play about this geeky little girl from Kansas. . . ."

Don't come, Jacob thought. This night will

be bad enough. Don't come, please don't come.
He looked at his sister. I'll give you money, he
thought, if you don't come.

"We'll all come," his mother said, a note of
finality in her voice. "It's the least we can do."

Perfect, Jacob thought, eating another spoon
of yogurt-pizza-garlic casserole. Everything ac-
cording to plan. My life is right back to blowing
up in my face.

Perfect.

13.

Love
Blossoms

AS disasters went for Jacob, this one started gently enough.

There was some initial madness before the play started, last minute running and thumping around on stage, Munchkins squealing and tearing back and forth, Mrs. Hilsak calling for order. None of this bothered Jacob. He had feathers in his stomach fluttering through the butterflies and the garlic-pizza-yogurt, but it wasn't anything to do with what was happening on top of the stage.

At last he was facing the fog machine head

on. It was time to use it, to get it ready to use, and he wasn't sure if he knew how to work it correctly.

First he had to pour in the solution, which smelled like a thick-sweet mouthwash.

Then he read the instructions.

Before emitting fog, the machine had to be pumped up with the handle on the top until the right amount of pressure was registered on a dial. He worked the pump handle but the dial didn't move. He pumped more, and still more without movement.

He began to sweat in the small place beneath the stage, though it wasn't hot. Above he heard sudden silence as the play started.

He pumped harder. Still nothing showed on the dial.

Dorothy and Toto had their difficulty with the crotchety old lady on the bike—also played by Maria. She even made being ugly beautiful, Jacob thought, listening to her above him, pumping frantically at the handle.

Suddenly the needle on the pressure dial slammed to the right.

He stopped pumping.

I wonder, he thought, what happens when

there is that much pressure? He looked for a way to let the pressure off without turning the fog machine on but there wasn't a valve. The dial didn't say how much pressure there was, only that it should be in the green area. It was well past the green and halfway around again.

Well, he thought. Well. Maybe that just means more fog.

So that was all right. The more fog that shot up out of the trapdoor when he opened it the better. The easier it would be for Maria to hide and lower herself. That was the logic he used but there was a nudge of worry in his brain. He chose to ignore it.

Up on top the cyclone hit and Dorothy awakened in the land of Oz and was meeting the Tin Woodsman and the Cowardly Lion and the Scarecrow. She sang "Over the Rainbow" then met the ugly witch.

Maria.

Oh my ugly witch, he thought—everything I ever wanted in a woman up on the the stage above me and I'm stuck with a fog machine that's going to explode. So stupid. I'm so stupid. None of this would be happening if I weren't so stupid.

Dorothy was captured in the castle. The ugly witch wanted the ruby slippers. Munchkins stomped around. Dorothy screamed. The Scarecrow and Lion and Woodsman saved her. Soon Dorothy would confront the Wicked Witch again.

It was coming now.

The ugly witch had to go.

It was time for the fog.

Timing was everything.

In one smooth motion he was supposed to turn on the fog machine and open the trap door. And he was ready.

Too ready.

His foot bumped against the leg of the fog machine and he tripped. As he started to fall forward his hand brushed the on-off switch on the fog machine and turned it on.

A full half a minute too soon.

There was a great, barfing "woof!" as the machine triggered. With a smell like an exploding mouthwash factory the throat of the fog machine began to blow out clouds, jets, rolling mountains of fog. It was thick, noxious, billowing. Jacob couldn't see, couldn't think. In two seconds the whole underside of the stage was filled, packed, and still the machine roared, fog pouring out. He had to get away.

He staggered, started to fall and grabbed overhead. His hand caught the bolt holding the trapdoor and it slid open.

The trapdoor dropped.

Fog blew up through the hole, exploded like a silent bomb, filled the stage. It was too much fog for the stage, too much for the theater, too much for the world, and panic took the Munchkins who were backstage and they began to run and scream. In seconds the fog and stampeding Munchkins had reached the audience and the panic infected them as well.

"It's smoke!" someone yelled. "Fire!"

All order, sense, intelligence, left the audience. Like a mad herd of water buffalo they wheeled, bellowed, screamed, and went for the exits, over the seats, over each other, fighting to get through the rolling clouds of fog still belching out of the hole in the stage and filling the auditorium.

But worse, far worse, Maria had been standing near the trapdoor and a galloping Munchkin bumped the front of her legs, pushing her backward. She tipped and dropped like a stone down, down into the hole, into the fog.

She screamed.

My love, Jacob raged, slashing in the thickness—my love is being attacked. The fog machine is attacking my love. Have to kill it.

Blinded now, he leapt for the machine, hit it with his shoulder, and knocked it over.

It only made things worse. The machine seemed to double its efforts, and now the fog was so thick he couldn't see his hands.

"Maria!" He screamed. "Where are you?"

"Here." She coughed, gagged. "Here. By the machine, I think."

He reached, missed, reached again, and found her shoulder near the floor where she had landed. Frantically he kneeled and wrapped his arm around her neck, as he would try to save a drowning person, and started crawling for where he thought the door should be. He was not thinking now, not thinking at all, but just clawing, pulling, trying to live, to save her.

"I was stupid," he rattled, crawling, pulling her. "I was stupid and just wanted to talk to you and all this happened, just wanted to stop you and talk to you in the hall and I almost hung myself and then I flew into a mountain trying to test a fighter . . ."

"Guurrrk." She choked, rasped. "Jacob . . ."

Screams came from the front of the auditorium. Vision was impossible. They were looking for the exits by feel.

". . . right into a mountain, just splattered all over and just because I wanted to talk to you and didn't dare, wanted to ask you for a date, ask you to go to a movie and didn't dare . . . and then the jocks got me, the jocks for pete's sake, got me and stuffed me in the garbage cans and I started to do math and all I wanted, all I wanted in the world was to take you to a movie . . ."

"Jacob." She pulled his hand down. "It's all right. Here's the door. It's all right." They scrabbled through the door and closed it.

". . . just wanted to take you to a movie and I didn't dare ask you, didn't dare do anything . . ."

"I'll go."

". . . because I'm stupid and shy and next it will be physics. . . . You'll what?"

"I said I'd go to the movie with you."

"You will?" He stared at her, astonished. Not

looking at her without looking at her, but actually *looking at her*. Right in the eyes.

She coughed the last of the fog out, nodded. "Sure. As a matter of fact I was going to ask you out if you didn't ask me."

"You were?"

"Yes."

"Why?"

"Because I like you."

"You do?"

"Yes."

"Why?"

"Is that all you're going to do—ask questions?"

"Me?"

"Yes, you. Don't you think we should do something about the fog?"

He remembered then. The machine. He had to turn off the machine. He had to go back in there and turn it off. He put his hand on the door then stopped, looked back at Maria. "Wait a minute. You mean you'll really go out with me?"

She nodded. "Sure."

He thought. "I mean not just maybe, but really? You really mean it?"

Another nod.

"Will you go to a movie with me next Friday night?" he insisted.

"Yes, yes, yes—now go turn off the machine before they lose the whole school in fog."

He opened the door. Billows of fog rolled out.

One week, he thought, vanishing in the gray muck. One week.

I've got one week to get my learner's permit, take the test, learn to drive, get my license, get my sister to like me and loan me her car.

Perfect.

14.
Love
Fulfilled

OR almost perfect.

"You have to take the driver's education class for nine hours before you can take the permit test," the driver's education teacher told him. "Then you have to get a license before you can actually take the car out alone. . . ."

"Can't I do it all in one day?" Jacob asked. "A long day?"

Not that it would have helped.

His sister didn't come to like him. Although that wasn't exactly the way she put it. He spent three days buttering her up, helping her clean her room, opening the door for her, not inter-rupting her when she was complaining, and it was all for nothing.

"The only way I would loan you my car," she said, looking at him incredibly beautifully with her beauty-contest eyes over a spoonful of chewy yogurt, which he had opened and handed to her, "is if you promised to drive it off a cliff."

I wish, Jacob thought, turning to leave, I had spit in the yogurt.

"Why do you want to borrow your sister's car?" his mother asked. They were in the kitchen and she was sipping a cup of coffee.

"Because the little toilet has a date," his sister said. "Somebody is actually going out with him."

"A date?" She put her cup down. "Well—couldn't I take you somewhere? The two of you?"

Oh great, he thought. My mother can take me on a date. Great.

And it was Friday.

Friday and he had no hope.

Maria met him in the hall in the afternoon just after gym class.

"What movie are we going to see tonight?"

She was wearing a T-shirt with something that looked like a dead dog or a sleeping burro on it and he thought he'd never seen anything so beautiful and he wanted to lie, wanted to tell her he had learned to drive and that his sister loved him and had given him the car, but he didn't.

"I can't take you on a date," he said, feeling the ground open up beneath his feet. "Nothing is right. I couldn't get a car and I don't know how to drive and . . ."

"That doesn't matter." She interrupted him.

"It doesn't?"

She shook her head. "Not at all. We don't need a car and you don't need to know how to drive. I have a motor scooter. I'll pick you up at six and we'll go to the movie."

Which is exactly the way it happened.

Except for the Doberman from Hell who chased them and almost caught part of Jacob that was sticking out over the back of the motor scooter and the fact that there was a long line at the movie so they didn't get in until the second show and they were out of buttered popcorn and about eighty-five thousand people saw them waiting and most of them were jocks and Jacob knew they would try to put him in the trash container the next day, not just try but do it, jam him right down into the trash and it all overwhelmed him and he turned to Maria and said it—didn't want to say it, hated to say it, hated his mouth for saying it but said it:

"Why are you going out with me?"

And she looked at him and smiled and he knew the smile was real, was gentle and real and she said: "Because you're a winner."

"I am?" he said, his voice quiet.

"Yes. Absolutely."

"Oh. I didn't know." And he thought then, finally, things were perfect.

Perfect.